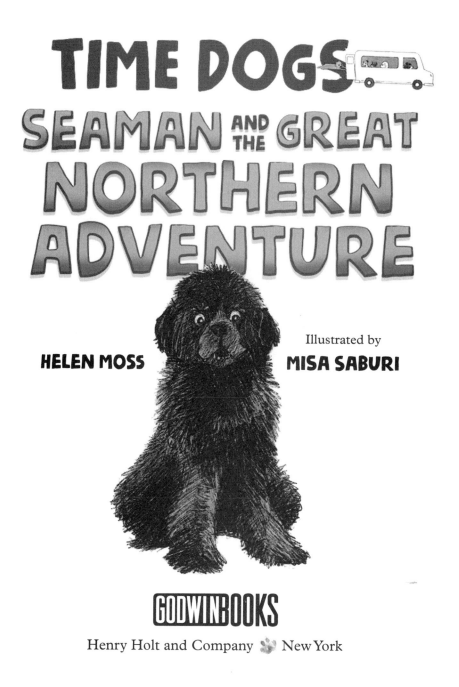

TIME DOGS

SEAMAN AND THE GREAT NORTHERN ADVENTURE

HELEN MOSS

Illustrated by
MISA SABURI

GODWINBOOKS

Henry Holt and Company 🐾 New York

Henry Holt and Company, *Publishers since 1866*
Henry Holt® is a registered trademark of Macmillan Publishing Group, LLC
175 Fifth Avenue, New York, NY 10010 • mackids.com

Library of Congress Control Number: 2018955698
ISBN 978-1-250-18635-5

Our books may be purchased in bulk for promotional, educational,
or business use. Please contact your local bookseller or the Macmillan
Corporate and Premium Sales Department at (800) 221-7945 ext. 5442
or by email at MacmillanSpecialMarkets@macmillan.com.

First edition, 2019 / Designed by April Ward
Printed in the United States of America by LSC Communications,
Harrisonburg, Virginia

1 3 5 7 9 10 8 6 4 2

TO MUM AND DAD

1

THE SQUEAKY, FREAKY FLYING MACHINE

I was woken by the whiff of rotting tuna.

I sat up and sniffed. The tuna smell was old cat food. I was also picking up hot sauce, wet carpet, and chicken poop. I may not be as quick on my paws as I used to be, but my nose is as sharp as ever.

Clatter, bang, clatter.

The noise was coming from the dog flap in the back door. I did a quick head count.

Baxter, Maia, and Newton were all with me on the rug by the fire. "Security alert!" I barked. "Action! Action!"

Baxter grunted in his sleep.

Maia opened one eye.

Newton didn't do anything. He's a little deaf these days.

I gave up and raced down the hall. "Stop right where you are!" I shouted. I slipped on the wooden floor. Scooting to a stop, I found myself nose-to-nose with Titch.

I should have known from the smell!

Titch is a stray, but she turns up at Happy Paws Farm most days. Usually around mealtimes. Right now, she was halfway through the dog flap. "What's up, Trevor?" she barked, almost knocking me out cold with a blast of tuna breath.

"What's up? *What's up* is that I was

having a nice quiet nap. Then *someone* started breaking the door down."

"Not my fault they make these dumb flaps so small!" Titch wiggled her huge head. Her raggedy ears bobbed up and down, but she was still stuck. The dog flap flipped up and smacked my nose. "I'm going on a road trip," she said. "Any of you old-timers want to tag along?"

Maia, Baxter, and Newton padded sleepily into the hall. About time! The house could have been invaded by pests by now; rats or raccoons, or—even worse—a *cat*.

"No, *thank you!*" Maia yawned. "We do *not* want to ride the garbage truck with you again, Titch."

"Relax, Princess Fluffybutt!" Titch laughed. "No garbage trucks this time. I'm talking about the squeaky, freaky flying machine."

Baxter's ears drooped. "You mean the *van?*"

"Speak up!" barked Newton. "Did someone say *van?* Have you forgotten what happened last time?"

By jiminy! How could any of us forget? Baxter had only climbed into the old van to look for his favorite tennis ball. The van started beeping and wobbling. I called the pack to action. We jumped aboard to rescue him. Next thing we knew, we were zooming into the sky . . .

"Aw, come on!" said Titch, bits of cat food spraying from her mouth. "What else do you have planned? An action-packed afternoon of dribbling in your sleep?"

Titch had a point. It was one of those long, rainy days when nothing much happens. Last time, the van took us to a place called Alaska, where we joined a team of sled dogs on a life-or-death mission. My tail sprang up. I was ready for another adventure. But then I remembered. Old Jim would be coming to fetch me soon. I couldn't gallivant off and leave my human all alone.

Newton tipped his head to one side, thinking. He's a border collie. He's the brains of the pack and he does a lot of thinking. "It *would* be interesting to see Balto and the team again," he said.

Baxter's ears perked up again. "And play in the snow . . ."

Maia did a little prance. "I have a dance class with Ayesha tonight, but I could squeeze in a short visit."

I made a pack decision. "Count us in," I told Titch. "As long as we're home by pickup time."

2

NO DOGS ALLOWED

Road trip!" whooped Titch. "Let's go!"
Then she remembered she was stuck in the
dog flap. "Can someone help me out here?"

Baxter gave a shove.
With a *clatter-flap-clatter*
and a loud grunt, Titch
shot back and fell over
on the doorstep. She's
missing a back leg;

balance is not her strong point. We all jumped through after her and dashed and splashed across the yard to the barn. The van was parked inside with the back doors wide open.

We scrambled aboard.

Newton made for the driver's seat and ran his nose over the shiny box beside the steering wheel. The *control panel*, he calls it. Shaking raindrops from my fur, I jumped up beside him. All of a sudden, the control panel sparked into life. Lights flashed, buzzers beeped. The air crackled with the smell of thunderstorms.

The van lurched from side to side.

"Oh yeah!" yelled Titch. "The freaky flying machine is on the move!"

"Wait!" cried Maia. "Where's Baxter?"

I ran to the door and looked out. Baxter

was standing outside the barn like a startled squirrel. "All aboard!" I barked.
"Remember the pack motto: Never Leave
a Dog Behind!"

"I thought the van would be parked
outside—like last time." Baxter's voice was
muffled by the tennis ball in his mouth.
Like most Labrador retrievers, he likes to
chew stuff—especially when he gets scared.

And he gets scared a lot. "We're not *allowed* in the barn," he whimpered.

So that's what this was about! Baxter lives at Happy Paws Farm full-time. The rest of us just stay here when our humans are busy. Baxter's humans, Lucy and her grandma, make *inventions* in the barn. Mostly shiny things that beep and zap and give you the heebie-jeebies. Point is, the barn is strictly No Dogs Allowed.

"Baxter, buddy!" Titch hollered over my shoulder. "We're not *in* the barn. We're *in* the van. It's a totally different thing."

At last, Baxter sprinted across the barn—with his eyes closed, as if that meant he wasn't really there—and jumped into the van.

Just in time.

The van lifted off the ground. Higher

and higher we rose. Past the inventions hanging from racks on the walls. Past the pigeons roosting in the rafters . . . Suddenly

Newton looked up. "Ah, we probably should have thought this through," he murmured. "We're *inside* the barn. We're going to crash into the roof . . . any . . . second . . . now . . ."

I braced, ready for the smash of solid van against solid roof.

But it didn't come. No crashing or smashing. Just a fizz that rippled through my fur. Then, somehow, we were out of the barn and zooming up through a dark, shimmery sky.

The back of the van is kitted out with furniture. Maia sat on the bed. Titch tried to open the refrigerator. I checked the corners for rats. Then I curled up by the doors to wait. When I woke, the van was rattling and creaking—just like it did last time. We began to plummet, down, down, down, faster and faster. "Hold your positions!" I barked. I stood to attention, my ears and tail held high. I like to set a good example to the pack; otherwise they can panic. Especially Baxter.

We hit the ground at last. *Thud, bump, scrape.*

I turned to Maia. She may be a fluffy little papillon, with pink ribbons and a sparkly pink collar, but she's a lot tougher than she looks. She's also done agility training. Maia is my go-to dog for special operations—like opening doors. "I'm on it," she said, standing on her back legs and pressing the handle on one of the doors with her paw.

"Look out, Alaska, here we come!"

Titch dove out through the doors, just as they flew open. "Last one in the snow has to kiss a cat on the nose!"

No one moved. We just stared out after her. We didn't want to kiss a cat, of course.

It's just that there *was* no snow.

3

DUCKZILLA!

Titch picked herself up and shook mud from her fur.

By jiminy! I thought. *Alaska sure has changed!* We had landed beside a wide river. Sunshine sparkled on the water. Plains of long, golden grass stretched away on either side.

"Most peculiar," Newton murmured. "It's winter at home. But it's summer here."

He frowned at the control panel. The lights had settled into a pattern of glowing lines:

1805

"I wonder what that means . . ."

I jumped down from the van to assess the situation. Closing my eyes, I searched the air for the scent of Balto and the sled team. A million thrilling smells crowded into my nostrils. I forgot all about *assessing*. Dizzy with excitement, I raced along the riverbank. Life of every kind was bursting out all around. Flocks of geese and ducks flew low over the water. Herds of antelope and elk grazed on the plains. The air buzzed with bugs and the grass rustled with small scurrying creatures.

My legs felt so springy I couldn't help jumping like a grasshopper.

Maia danced in a cloud of yellow butterflies.

Baxter splashed through shoals of shimmering fish.

Titch rolled in a giant cow pie.

Even Newton quit *wondering* and joined the fun, rounding up rabbits, chipmunks, and squirrels.

All of a sudden, I remembered: this happened last time we came to Alaska, too. We had changed from "old-timers" to puppies again.

I wanted to explore everything at once. Nests, burrows, droppings, trails . . . But then something stopped me in my tracks. "Alert! Alert!" I called. "Attention All Pack!"

"You won't catch many rats making all that noise!" Newton laughed. Now that he was a puppy, his ears were working again. I guess everything sounded extra loud to him.

But it wasn't rats I was worried about. It was the trail of fresh paw prints. For a moment, I thought it was Balto. The prints smelled like *dog*. They looked like *dog* . . . and yet . . . Titch placed a huge front paw inside one of them. There was room to spare.

And it wasn't just the size of the prints that puzzled me. The shape was odd, too. The pads were kind of *joined together.*

Newton peered at them. "This dog appears to have *webbed* paws like a duck or a goose. Hmm . . . most interesting."

Titch's fur stood on end. "That's not *interesting!*" she shrieked. "That's a freak of nature. Half dog, half duck!" She bared her teeth and whipped around. "Where are you hiding, *Duckzilla*? You don't scare me!"

Baxter shrank away, looking around for his tennis ball, but he'd dropped it when he was splashing in the river. "It's a *m-m-mon-ster!*" he wailed.

I had to get the pack under control. "Don't panic," I said. "There's no such thing as monst–*oomph!*"

That *oomph* was the sound I made as something very big, very black, and very shaggy leaped out from a thornbush and landed on top of me.

4

THE WRONG TRAIL

"**A**aagh!" I yelped.

"AAAGGH!" roared the thing, as it sprang away from me.

Baxter peeped out from behind Newton. "Is it going . . . to . . . eat . . . us?"

Newton shook his head. "It's just a dog!"

"Of course I'm a *dog*," said the giant dog in a deep, rumbly voice. "What did you think I was?"

Maia flicked her ears "A monst—"

"A monstrous *bear*," I cut in. This guy would take us for a bunch of nincompoops if he thought we believed in *monsters*. I bowed politely, trying to give a good first impression of my pack.

The dog began to sniff us over. Then he noticed we were all staring at his webbed paws. "You pups never met a Newfoundland before?" he asked. "Kings of the Water, they call us. We swim like fish, swift and strong."

"Show-off!" muttered Titch. She had no time for good impressions. "So, *Duckzilla*," she snarled. "What's the big idea? Leaping out at people like that?"

The Newfoundland shook his head. "*Duck-zilla?* Seems you've mistaken me for someone else. My name's Seaman. From the Lewis and Clark tribe. Who are you pups with? The Hidatsa? Arikara? One of the Sioux nations?"

Baxter and Maia stared at him, their mouths hanging open. Even Newton looked puzzled.

Titch broke off from scratching at a mosquito bite on her butt. "We're with the flying van, buddy."

"The *Fly-Ing-Van?*" Seaman repeated. "Nope, never heard of them. Well, anyways, sorry about jumping out at you." He sniffed suspiciously in Titch's direction. "Reckon I mistook you for a buffalo."

Titch growled at him. "Do I *look* like a buffalo?"

Seaman shrugged. "No, but you sure do smell like one."

Maia giggled. "So *that's* what the giant cow pie was!"

But Seaman was already heading off into the long grass. "Can't stand here shooting the breeze all day," he called back. "Work to do. One of my humans wandered off yesterday. Gotta find him."

I shouted after him, "Yesterday, you say?"

"Yup!" said Seaman, without turning around. "Went off hunting. Didn't come back."

"You're on the wrong trail, then! The scent you're following *is* human, but it's old." I sniffed the grass. "At least five days, I'd say."

Titch blocked Seaman's path, standing as firm as her three legs would allow. "So, here's the deal, Duckzilla," she said. "We help you find your human. You give us an all-you-can-eat dinner at your place."

Seaman pushed past her, but Titch didn't give up. "Go on, Trev. Do your thing."

I don't take orders from Titch, of course. But there's nothing I love more than a good tracking mission. Nose down, tail up, I set to work. It didn't take long to pick up another human scent. *Wood smoke. Gunpowder. Grease.* Less than a day old, too. I locked my nostrils onto the trail and pushed through the tangle of young willow trees along the riverbank. The others raced after me.

"Help!"

I looked around. A big round face was peeping out from the branches of a mighty cottonwood. A human face.

"Yup, that's York," said Seaman, pulling up next to me. "What the blazes is he doing up there?"

We soon found out. A creature the size of a truck burst out of the bushes and charged at the tree.

Suddenly it caught our scent and swung around to face us.

Fear and excitement chased each other up and down my spine.

This time it really was a bear.

5

NOW OR NEVER

Doggone it!" muttered Seaman. "It's a grizzly."

The grizzly bear snarled, showing us his yellow fangs. His small black eyes glinted with rage. But it was the human he wanted. He reared up, threw back his head, and roared. Then he smashed his front paws down onto the trunk of the cottonwood tree. Again and again, the grizzly struck. The tree swayed and creaked under the relentless attack.

A patch of dark blood matted the fur on the bear's shoulder. "Looks like York got a shot at him," said Seaman.

No wonder the bear was mad, I thought.

Newton pointed at a long wooden object lying in the grass. "He's dropped his gun."

A branch crashed to the ground. "HELP!" the man cried.

Seaman cussed under his breath and began creeping toward the bear. "I'm going in," he said.

I stood to attention. "We'll provide backup. It's our pack duty to help out a fellow dog."

"Are you totally *nuts*?" Titch snorted.

"That monster will chew you up and spit
you out like one of Baxter's tennis balls."

"Wait!" said Newton. "I have an idea.
We all charge at the bear from different

directions at exactly the same time. He'll be so confused, it'll give the human time to jump down from the tree and get away."

"*Charge?*" Baxter gulped. "As in *run?* *Toward* the bear? That sounds s-s-scary."

"It's simple if you get the timing right," said Maia. "Just like a dance move."

Seaman stopped creeping. "All right. We'll give it a try. You pups get into position and wait for my signal."

It was a good plan. But who did Seaman think he was, giving orders to my pack? That was my job. I bit back my frustration and waited for his signal. *Crash!* Another branch broke. By jiminy! What was Seaman waiting for? It was now or never. "Pack, *attack!*" I barked. "Go! Go! Go!"

I charged at the bear.

Behind me I heard Seaman shout.

"No, not yet! I'm not ready!"

But there was no turning back now.

A giant paw was coming straight at me.

6

THE RIGHT MOMENT

I twisted away. Just in time. Claws as long as knives sliced tufts of fur from my side. The grizzly took another swipe. I tried to dodge again. I stumbled and fell. Those deadly claws were almost at my throat when I saw a flash of fluffiness racing toward me.

"Maia! Get back!" I yelled.

But the bear had seen her, too. At the last moment, the giant paw swerved away from me and batted Maia high into the air. Then it swept at me again. This time I was ready. I leaped onto the back of the paw. The bear roared and raised his paw to his mouth, trying to bite me. I sprang past the long yellow fangs and landed on top of the bear's nose. Clinging on tight, I dug my teeth and claws into the soft flesh of his snout.

The bear squealed in pain. Blood filled my mouth. I didn't know whether it was mine or the bear's. I couldn't hold on much longer. But if this was the end, I would go out fighting.

And now, at last, the others were joining the battle. Newton, Baxter, and Seaman rushed in, barking and gnashing their teeth. The bear spun around, swatting them away like mosquitoes.

Crack! The gunshot split the sky in two. The man must have escaped from the tree and found his gun. He fired again. The smell of gunpowder filled the air. The shots missed, but the bear took fright. With a grunt of defeat, he dropped to all fours and lumbered away.

I jumped clear and rolled into a bush. When I opened my eyes, three faces were peering down at me. Newton and Baxter looked worried. Seaman looked furious. "You harebrained maniac!" he bellowed. "You could have gotten us all killed! I said *I'd* give the signal . . ."

"You were too slow," I snapped.

Seaman growled in frustration. "I was waiting for the right moment. You, young pup, should have done the same."

"It *was* the right moment. The moment *before* the bear shook the man from the tree and ate him for dinner!" I sat up and looked around. "Where's Maia?" I gasped, suddenly remembering the bear throwing her into the air . . .

"I'm right here!" Maia's voice came from near the tree. She was busy smoothing down her fur. "I did an awesome double backflip and landed on a branch." She sighed. "Don't tell me no one saw it."

"I was kind of busy," I muttered. I tried to sound mad at her. Really, I was just relieved.

"Don't fight, guys!" Baxter wagged his

tail. "Newton's genius plan worked. The bear has gone. The human is safe."

"Oh yeah! Go, us!" Titch strolled out from behind a rock.

"*Us?*" I spluttered. Now I really *was* mad. "Tell me. What exactly did *you* do?"

"Relax, Trev!" Titch tossed her head. "*Someone* had to keep a lookout. In case Old Grizzly's bear buddies showed up to join the fight."

I looked at Newton, Baxter, and Maia. We couldn't help laughing. If Titch had a pack motto, it would be Look After Number One.

I heard a noise and whipped around. But it was only the man, York. Water dripped from his clothes. He must have jumped in the river, in case the bear chased him.

"Goodboy!" he said, scooping me up in his arms. "You led the charge, didn't you?" Then he patted Seaman and the others. "Good job, everyone."

Titch butted her head against Seaman's shoulder. "We've kept our side of the deal," she said. "Now how about that dinner you owe us?"

7

GOODBOY, HERO

Seaman led us back along the riverbank. He'd stuck to the deal and agreed to give us a meal. But he was still furious. He marched ahead, swishing his tail like an angry cat.

All of a sudden, he caught sight of the van parked on the bank. He backed away, his ears clamped down in fright. Then, with a soft *pop*, the van turned into an old willow tree. By now, Seaman had a serious case of the heebie-jeebies. "What the blazes," he mumbled. "Your *Fly-Ing-Van* tribe sure has some *powerful* magic . . ."

"It's just camouflage," Newton explained. "The van changes to match the background. It was a snowy rock last time we came to Alaska. Now it's a tree . . ."

A pair of crows landed in the branches and cawed at us.

Seaman wrinkled his nose suspiciously. "It doesn't *smell* like a tree . . ."

He was right, of course. The van smelled exactly like a van.

"I've figured that part out," said Newton. "The van is a human invention. Humans can't smell. If it *looks* like a tree, they think it's a tree. The camouflage works. They don't notice the scent is wrong."

As if to prove the point, York walked right past the old willow without giving it a second glance.

A few more miles and we came to a bend in the river. "This is it!" said Seaman. "The Lewis and Clark camp."

We were looking down from a low cliff. Below us, on a wide beach of smooth, flat stones, humans were bustling in and out of

small shelters made of long poles and elk and buffalo skins. A cloud of wood smoke swirled around them like fog. I thought at first that it was one big family. Then I saw that they were all adult males, but for one female. She knelt beside the fire, stirring a cooking pot and singing to the baby on her back.

Two of the men hurried to meet us. One clapped York on the shoulder. The other—a tall, thin man with a long nose and kind eyes—crouched next to Seaman. Seaman gazed up at him. "This is my human, Captain Lewis," he said proudly. "He's the leader." He looked over at the man talking to York. "And that's Captain Clark. Second-in-command."

York scooped me up again. "This little fellow saved my life." York was a big man

with a very loud voice, and he was bellow-
ing in my ear. But I could tell he was saying
good things about me, so I licked his nose.
"I'm going to call him Hero. Goodboy,
Hero."

Hero. York said that word so many times I realized he thought it was my name. "No, I'm Trevor," I barked. "Tre-vor!"

York laughed and said *Hero* again.

"He can call you Cat-Poop-Face for all I care," said Titch. "As long as we get some food."

The woman by the fire—Seaman told us her name was Sacagawea—seemed to understand. She called us over to a pile of buffalo bones and fat. Fighting off grizzly bears is hungry work. We fell on that meal like a pack of wolves—even Maia, the world's pickiest eater.

"*Yum,*" slurped Baxter.

"*Yum,*" slurped Newton.

"*Yum . . . yum . . . yum!*" slurped Titch. Grease dribbled from her jowls. "Just needs . . . *slurp* . . . a little . . . *slurp* . . . hot sauce."

Full at last, I flopped down to lick my whiskers clean. Then I sprang up again. Mosquitoes were dive-bombing me from every direction. I hopped about, flicking my ears and snapping my teeth. "Is that an after-dinner dance?" Seaman laughed. The meal had clearly put him in a better mood. "Lie down by the fire," he said. "Doggone bugs can't stand the smoke."

I moved so close that the flames scorched my fur. The others joined me. *We should start for home soon*, I thought. Our humans would be coming to pick us up from Happy Paws. But I could barely keep my eyes open. "Just a short nap," I murmured. "Then back . . . to . . . the . . . van."

When I woke, the birds were settling down to roost in the trees. The humans sat cleaning their guns and mending clothes.

There were no flashes or beeps. I guessed they'd left their electrical things at home. The woman was braiding Maia's fur with beads and shells. "We came to visit our friend Balto," Baxter was saying to Seaman. "You must know him. He's famous in Alaska."

"Nope, never heard of any Balto." Seaman nibbled at a thorn in his paw. "Nor Alaska, neither. It must be upriver a ways." He gazed toward the distant mountains, a dreamy look on his face. The setting sun painted the snowy peaks red and pink. "That's where we're heading. Up the Missouri River and over the mountains, all the way to"—Seaman lowered his voice dramatically, as if he was about to say something wild and crazy—"the *Pacific Ocean*."

"In *those* tubs?" Titch laughed, glancing at the row of big wooden canoes tied up along the shore. "Why don't you guys just jump on the freeway? You could be hitting the surf this time tomorrow."

"I was wondering the same thing." Newton tipped his head to one side. "Where have your humans parked their cars?"

"*Free-way? Cars?*" Seaman looked around nervously, as if strange objects might appear out of thin air. "Are those a part of your *Fly-Ing-Van* magic, too?"

Baxter's mouth dropped open. I knew how he felt. Seaman *had* to be joking. How could he not know about cars?

I was about to ask.

But my words were lost in a thunderous clamor of hooves.

8

DANGEROUS!

The hooves belonged to a herd of antelope.

The frightened animals were stampeding across the plain, heading straight for the river. One after another, they began to hurl themselves over the cliff.

"They're running from a wolf pack," shouted Seaman, over the thunder of hooves and the *splash-crash* of antelope hitting the water. They were some way upriver from the camp, but still the noise was deafening. "Let's have ourselves some fun!" he cried, leaping up and running off along the beach toward them. "We'll race them across the river."

Baxter bounded after him, whooping with glee. Newton followed. He's not much of a swimmer, but his border collie instincts couldn't resist the chance to round up all those antelope.

Titch didn't move. "Water! *Gross!* If dogs were meant to swim, we'd have fins!"

Maia agreed. "I don't want to get my new braids all tangled."

I prefer to keep my paws on dry land, too. The three of us climbed to the top of the cliff and settled down on a flat rock to watch the race. The antelope were swimming for their lives, their heads held high above the water. Baxter was not far behind them. Newton had barely made it out of the shallows.

But Seaman was the star of the show! He surged past Baxter, dove under him, popped up on the other side, twisted around, then dove again. Onshore, the Newfoundland was like a big woolly bear. In water, he was as swift and sleek as a seal.

Maia wagged her tail admiringly. "Wow, those webbed paws are really something."

But Titch just yawned. "What a show-off!"

With a bark of excitement, Seaman glided alongside a young antelope near the back of the herd. All of a sudden, dog and antelope both sank beneath the surface.

The water churned and frothed.

Swirls of blood billowed through it.

Maia gasped. "I thought this was a race. Why is Seaman *attacking* that antelope?"

Now, I'm a Jack Russell terrier. I'm a born hunter. But even I didn't think it was fair to bring down a terrified animal just for fun. It wasn't a pest, and we didn't need it for food.

But it wasn't Seaman who popped back

up through the bubbling water. It was the antelope. Eyes rolling in fear, long legs thrashing, it kept on swimming for shore.

I scanned the river for Seaman.

At last his nose broke up through the ripples. "Help!" he howled. "It bit me!"

"Bitten by an antelope?" Titch laughed. "Ooh, *dangerous*! If you're a blade of grass, that is."

But the blood was now a dark, spreading cloud.

And Seaman had disappeared beneath the water once more.

9

LOOK BEFORE YOU LEAP

I quickly assessed the situation. Luckily, Baxter was not far from the spot where the cloud of blood still swirled. "Baxter!" I shouted. "Danger! Danger! Seaman's in trouble."

"I'm on it!" barked Baxter, speeding to the place where Seaman had disappeared. He dove. He surfaced. "It's a beaver!" he yelled. "It's got hold of Seaman's leg."

Baxter dove again. When he came back up, he was dragging Seaman with him, his teeth clamped around the big dog's shaggy scruff.

Maia cheered. "Hooray for Baxter!"

I was proud of him, too. Baxter is scared of his own shadow, but he can be brave when it matters most. We learned that when we were helping the sled team in Alaska.

But it was too soon to celebrate. The water churned and Seaman vanished again. "The beaver won't let go," Baxter spluttered. "It keeps pulling him down."

I knew what I had to do. Baxter is the top dog for water-based rescue operations. But if it came down to a fight, he didn't stand a chance. Labradors are just too gentle for their own good. This was a job for a terrier. "Hang in there," I shouted. "I'm coming!" I ran along the cliff top to the point where the beach below narrowed to a thin strip. I could jump straight into the water from here. Maia was right behind me, ready to dive in, too, but I had a better idea. "Go alert the humans," I told her. "We might need them."

As always in a crisis, Titch was nowhere to be seen.

I looked down at the river below. It ran deep and swift and fierce. I gritted my teeth and closed my eyes. *Never Leave a Dog Behind*, I told myself. *Even if that dog did call you a harebrained maniac . . .*

"Wait!"

I opened my eyes. Newton was paddling toward Baxter and Seaman. "Look before you leap!" he shouted up at me. "The current has caught them . . . it's bringing them . . . closer to you." Newton panted out the words as he battled upriver. "If you time it right . . . you can land . . . next to them."

I looked back to where I'd last sighted Baxter. When his head appeared again, he was still clinging onto Seaman's scruff. All my instincts told me to leap into action. But Newton was right. They were drifting closer, blood trailing after them like a banner. Soon they would be right below me. I could dive-bomb the beaver. Take it by surprise.

I forced myself to wait . . .

and wait . . .

and then I leaped.

There was a moment of confusion; frothing water, thrashing paws, choking, spluttering. Then I felt something solid beneath me. Had I landed on a rock? But no, it was moving. I was on the beaver's back! It was a female, and even through the water, I could smell her fear and rage. Without stopping to think, or even breathe, I sank my teeth into her thick leathery tail and shook it for all I was worth.

Blood and water rushed up my nose and

into my throat. I hung on tight. The beaver flailed her tail so hard I thought my jaws would snap. Just when I thought I couldn't hold on another moment, the beaver let go of Seaman's leg.

But the danger wasn't over. Ripping her tail from my jaws, she surged back up at me from below, aiming her huge bloodred teeth at my belly.

I kicked out hard and knocked her back.

The beaver gave up the fight at last. She rolled over and swam away.

I broke through the surface, gasping for air. Baxter was still holding Seaman up by his scruff. Newton had reached us now, too. We both grabbed some loose fur in our teeth to help Baxter. Seaman's eyes were closed. I wasn't even sure he was alive.

Baxter didn't look much better. "Keep swimming!" I mumbled. "Gotta . . . swim . . . to the shore . . ."

"It's no good," Newton panted. "The current's too powerful. It keeps sucking us back into the middle of the river."

10

NO OTHER OPTIONS

Seaman's eyes fluttered open. "*Snag . . . ,*" he murmured. "*Snag . . . current . . .*"

I did a furious snort that Titch would have been proud of. We'd been savaged half to death by a blood-crazed beaver, and now we were about to drown. This was more than a snag. It was a major crisis.

"*Snag . . . current . . . rock . . . willow . . .*"

Seaman had clearly lost his mind.

But suddenly Newton barked. "Of course! I know what Seaman's trying to say. He's telling us to work *with* the current. See those rocks in the middle of the river? If we steer that way, the current will carry us through the gap between them. It's like a mini waterfall. It comes out just above a big willow that's fallen across the river. I saw it earlier. That's what he means by a *snag*. It's a fallen tree. He reckons it will catch us."

"Will it work?" Baxter's voice was muffled by soggy fur.

Newton took a long time to reply. "Probably . . ."

I didn't like that word. What would happen if the snag *didn't* catch us? We would *probably* be swept miles downriver. We would *probably* drown. But there were no other options. I gave the order. "Hold tight and head for the rocks!"

Clinging on to Seaman's scruff, we paddled toward the middle of the Missouri with all the strength we had left. Soon the current had us in its grasp, flinging us at the rocks. Somehow, we made it through the narrow gap. Round and round we spun, water crashing over us, rocks bashing into us, as we tumbled along on the torrent. At last I heard Maia's voice. "Over here!" she barked. "This way!"

I heard Sacagawea shouting, too. "Seaman! Hero!"

I glimpsed them standing on the fallen willow trunk. Then I was underwater again. Something hit me across the back. We had washed up against the snag. We'd made it!

I heard a splintering crack.

A splash. The cry of a human pup.

The tree trunk had broken.

11

BAD ATTITUDE

I opened my eyes to darkness filled with the sounds and smells of sleeping humans and dogs. I was inside one of the shelters in the camp, tucked up on a warm blanket. But how did I get here? Where was my pack? Had I checked the corners for rats? "What happened?" I murmured.

The others were curled up next to me. Maia spoke softly. "Don't you remember,

Trevor? Seaman was bitten by a beaver . . ."

The memories flooded back. The current, the rocks, the snag. The terrible crack as the willow trunk broke.

"The humans got there just in time," said Newton. "They waded into the river and fished us out."

Baxter laughed. "We were like a bunch of big furry salmon! What a catch!"

Everyone was safe! Relief washed over me. But there was someone missing! "Where's Seaman?" I asked. "Did he make it?"

"Come and see." Newton led the way to the back of the tent. Seaman was lying on a pile of furs near Captain Lewis's bed. His injured back leg was wrapped in bandages, but his chest rose and fell with slow, wheezy breaths. He was alive!

"Captain Lewis carried him out of the water," whispered Baxter. As if hearing his name, Lewis stirred in his sleep. He reached out and patted Seaman's side.

I wagged my tail, even though it hurt. "We did a good job today, pack!" I said proudly. "Baxter, Newton, awesome rescue work. And Maia, too. You fetched the humans just in time."

Maia looked down. "But I didn't," she mumbled. "I shouted at them like crazy. But only Sacagawea followed me to the river. The men just hollered at me to be quiet."

"Can't say I blame them." Titch had appeared out of nowhere, a buffalo leg bone held in her jaws. "No offense, Princess Fluffybutt, but you do have an annoying, yappy little bark."

I should have been used to Titch and her bad attitude by now, but this was too much. "What is it with you, Titch?" I snarled. "I know you're not an official pack member. But you could help out once in a while! We could all have drowned. And where were you? *Looking After Number One* as usual."

Maia gently cuffed my nose with her paw. "But Titch *did* help out this time."

I gaped at her in surprise.

"That's right." Titch looked up from gnawing on the bone. "You tell Captain Hero. It was me who fetched the men."

Baxter laughed. "Well, you do have a *very* loud bark."

"I didn't just bark at them, buddy. I used the old Swipe and Run trick."

"The Swipe and Run trick?" I couldn't help asking.

Titch grinned. "You run off with one of the humans' favorite toys. Gets their attention every time. I usually go for those phone things they all love, but they don't have them here. So I swiped York's gun. You should have seen him sprint after me. All the way to the riverbank. He saw you goofballs in the water, and the woman with the baby standing on the willow trunk. He

called the other men . . ." Titch paused, crunching the bone in half. "They got there just as the snag broke."

I suddenly remembered the splash and the human cry. "The baby! He fell in the water!"

Newton nodded. "You won't believe this! Titch rescued him, too."

Titch shrugged. "No big deal. I was standing in the shallows watching all the drama, when the human pup just about landed on top of me. I picked it up and dropped it on the bank. Wriggly, squeaky little thing it is, too!"

There was a low groan. Seaman was opening his eyes. "Thank you," he murmured sleepily. "All of you." He lifted his head. "Trevor, I'm sorry I chewed you out before about charging at the bear. I'm *glad* you rushed in like a harebrained maniac this time. You saved my life."

Seaman was wrong, of course. I *hadn't* rushed in. I had wanted to. I was about to leap straight into the river. But I had listened to Newton's advice. I hung tight on the rock until Seaman and Baxter and the beaver were right below me. "I didn't exactly rush in," I said. "Thanks to Newton, I waited for the right moment. Just like you told me."

Seaman nodded seriously. "Well, I guess there are times to rush in, and times to hold back. The hard part is knowing which is which."

"Wise words, Duckzilla," said Titch. "And there are times *not* to show off by racing antelope too close to a beaver dam."

Seaman laughed. "That's the best advice I've heard in a long time." Then he winced in pain. "I thought I had lost this leg. Doggone beaver just about bit right through it. But Captain Lewis used his magic medicine, and he sewed it right up."

I was drifting off to sleep again. We would leave at first light, I decided. Head back to the van . . . and home . . .

But Seaman's next words jolted me awake. "How would you pups feel about staying to help take care of my humans while my leg heals?"

12

TALL TALES

Newton, Baxter, and Maia were not keen on staying. Newton has a big human family with a new baby to look after. Baxter has his girl, Lucy, and all of Happy Paws Farm to protect. Maia's human lady, Ayesha, can't manage without her.

I felt the same way. Old Jim's mate, Brenda, died last year, and he needs me more than ever. But Seaman had asked for our help. It was our pack duty to do what we could. "How about two days?" I said. "Three, max."

"I'll hang around as long as you like," said Titch. "Buffalo meat is awesome."

Seaman looked up at me. "Thank you. I reckon three days will be time enough to rest my leg. Then you can return to your *Fly-Ing-Van* people."

"It's a deal," I said.

Next morning, after an early breakfast, Captain Lewis gave orders for the men to pack up camp. Then we set off. Some of the humans rode in the boats, while others hiked along the riverbank.

We soon settled into our new jobs. Maia

kept watch over Sacagawea and the baby. Newton worked with Captain Clark, scouting out the trail ahead. Baxter took Seaman's place alongside Captain Lewis, happily diving into the river to fetch the ducks and geese that he shot. I teamed up with York, who also loved to hunt. We tracked down everything from prairie dogs to porcupines. I was having so much fun as Hero I almost forgot my old life as Trevor.

Titch didn't help out at all, of course. "Humans are seriously overrated," she said. Instead, she rode in one of the canoes, with Seaman. To my surprise, they quickly became firm friends. They called themselves the Three-Legged Club and spent all day swapping stories. Before he met Captain Lewis, Seaman was a ship's dog. Titch had also been to sea—as a stowaway on a cruise ship. Now and then, I listened in to their tall tales. Seaman, it seemed, had fought off pirates and ferocious sea monsters. Titch had chased mermaids and been half eaten by a giant shark.

The rest of us had no time for stories. We were too busy trying to keep the humans alive.

There was danger everywhere. The very next night a startled buffalo charged toward the camp. It would have crushed the men who were sleeping outside by the fire, if I hadn't raised the alarm. We barked and growled at that buffalo until, at the last moment, it changed direction and galloped away into the night.

Then there was the wildcat. A huge, ferocious beast with a spotted coat and tufted ears. It leaped from a tree and landed on York, savagely clawing his back. I soon scared it off by biting its tail. There were narrow escapes from coyotes, wolves, and rattlesnakes, too.

Wild animals were not the only hazards. There were grass fires on the plains and mudslides on the cliffs. There were hailstones the size of coconuts. Late on the second day, a strong wind began to blow, whipping the river into foaming waves. The men put up sails and the canoes raced along on the breeze. All of a sudden, a gust of wind caught the boat that Titch and Seaman were riding in and spun it around.

The boat hit a wave side-on. It lurched and swayed and almost flipped right over.

Somehow the boat stayed upright.

But it was filling with water and sinking fast.

13

THE MAGIC NOSE

Hearing the commotion, York and I ran to the riverbank.

The two brave sea dogs of the Three-Legged Club were clinging to the sinking canoe, howling for help. Seaman couldn't swim with his bandaged leg, and I suspect that Titch—for all her tales of chasing mermaids and fighting sharks—could not swim at all.

Some of the men on the boat began bailing out the water with pots and pans. Others rowed frantically for the shore. Newton and Maia were on board, too, along with Sacagawea. Maia helped her grab the boxes of supplies that were being washed away, while Newton kept a tight hold on the baby.

Baxter and Captain Lewis hurried along the cliff top to join us. "The compass!" cried Lewis. "Save the compass!"

I didn't understand the human words, but Lewis was pointing at a small flat wooden box in the water below. Maia balanced on the bow of the boat and reached down to scoop it up, but a wave snatched it out of her mouth. Up and up it flew. Down it dropped, toward the bottom of the cliff.

If the little box landed on the rocks, it would surely smash to pieces.

But instead of a smash, we heard a soft thud and a startled honk.

The box had fallen into the nest of a very angry goose.

Captain Lewis began to climb down the cliff.

"Come back!" Baxter barked at him in alarm. "The cliff's not safe. It's crumbling."

But it was too late. Lewis was already slipping. He slid to a stop on a narrow ledge, stones tumbling down all around him. One wrong move and he would plummet onto the rocks below. York took a coil of rope from his belt and began to lower it down the cliff.

Meanwhile, the goose had pushed the little box out of the nest and was nudging it toward the water with his beak. I scrambled down the cliff and onto the rocks. "Hand over the box!" I barked. "It belongs to my humans."

The furious goose honked rude words at me. He also flapped his wings and stabbed at me with his beak. Titch had named Seaman Duckzilla, but this was *Goose*zilla. Dodging the deadly beak, I snatched up the box in my teeth and ran for my life.

I sped back up the cliff, just in time to see York and Baxter pull Captain Lewis up over the edge. Lewis flopped onto the grass. "The compass!" he groaned, thumping his head in frustration.

I dropped the wooden box onto his chest. Captain Lewis grabbed it, flipped the top open, and looked inside. He tapped it a few times and then laughed.

I could tell the man was happy, so I wagged my tail. York knelt and stroked my ears. "Goodboy, Hero!"

I wagged my tail even more.

Later, when the boat was safely on dry land
and we were all sitting by the fire, I asked
Seaman why that little wooden box was so
important to the humans.

"It contains the Magic Nose," he said.

"*Magic Nose?*" I repeated in surprise. I was learning that Seaman saw magic just about everywhere.

Seaman nodded. "That's right. You know how humans can't smell? When they want to figure out which way to go, they can't just pick up a scent the way we do. Well, Captain Lewis uses the Magic Nose to sniff the air and find scents for him. He checks it just about every time we set off."

"Oh, I get it. It's a *compass*!" Newton laughed. "My humans use one when we go for hikes." He shook his head at Seaman. "It's not really magic. It's a kind of human invention."

Baxter's ears suddenly drooped. I could tell that the word *invention* had reminded him of his girl, Lucy, and her grandma. He was missing them.

I was missing home, too. I loved being Hero, out hunting all day with York. But I needed a rest. I was ready to be Trevor again, snoozing with Old Jim in our favorite armchair. I nudged Baxter's nose with mine. "Seaman's leg is healing fast. We'll go home soon."

Newton wagged his tail. "Good. This place is too dangerous. It's life or death every other moment. I'm a nervous wreck!"

"Protecting these humans is a full-time

job," said Maia. "I'm ready to go home to Ayesha." She scratched at a bead in her fur. "And I miss my coconut shampoo. These braids are starting to itch."

We didn't know that the biggest danger still lay ahead.

And it came from the humans themselves.

14

NOTHING BUT TROUBLE

The next day, some miles upriver from the Magic Nose Rescue, a small group of men on horseback came galloping up behind us, followed by a ragtag pack of skinny dogs. The men slid down from their horses and walked along the bank to talk to our humans, who were tying up the boats for the night.

While Seaman stuck to Captain Lewis's

side, I hurried over to the new dogs to carry out a security check. They were already scarfing down a pile of fish guts our men had dumped in the shallow water. "State your names and your business here," I barked, raising my tail high to show them I was in charge.

Their leader was an old mud-brown female with even more bits missing than Titch. "Back off!" she snarled, crouching over the fish guts, her hackles flicking up

like knives. Her teeth were as thin and jagged as those of an eel.

I yelped. In pain, not in fear. Baxter was hiding behind me and had started chewing nervously on my tail.

Another dog pushed forward. "Hey! They're just a bunch of puppies playing at being tough guys!" They all laughed, fish blood spraying from their long, pointed muzzles.

"I'm Fang, if you must know," said the leader. "We're not here to make trouble, kid. Seems to me you have more than enough food to go around." She aimed a look at Baxter. He'd eaten a large elk steak for lunch, and his belly was as round as a barrel.

Titch growled. "Just keep your gnashers off the buffalo meat. That's ours!"

"What about your humans?" Maia chipped in, before Titch could start a fight. "Are they good men?"

"*Good?* How should I know? We're wild dogs, not *pets.*" Fang sneered at Maia's beads and feathers and her pink collar. "We're just tagging along with them awhile for the free food." She glanced at the new pack of men. "That tall one with the beard is their boss, Larocque. From what we can pick up from the horses, they've been trading in all the villages along the river. For beaver furs, mainly. They're heading home, way over the plains to the north."

"North?" said Newton hopefully. "Not Alaska, by any chance?"

Fang shrugged. "Never heard of it."

"All clear! The humans have made

friends," said Seaman, strolling over to join us. "Captain Lewis has invited them to stay the night in our camp." He looked down at Fang. "We're on a mission to find the Pacific Ocean," he barked importantly.

"Whatever!" Fang buried her nose in the fish guts again. "We're on a mission to eat this lot before the rats show up."

That evening the humans threw a party. They built a big fire and sat around eating mountains of buffalo meat, which smelled delicious, and drinking whiskey, which did not. They talked and laughed and played cards. Some took out fiddles and made the screechy noises humans seem to like so much.

We settled down to the never-ending

task of removing grass seeds from our fur. I invited Fang and her pack to join us by the fire. Although it was summer, the night air was crisp and cold. But the wild dogs refused to set paw inside the camp. "You shouldn't get too cozy with humans, kid," warned Fang. "They are nothing but trouble."

Looking back, maybe she had a point.

But it wasn't the visitors who started it. It was men from our own pack. Reed and Newman had been helping themselves to extra rations from the whiskey barrel. Seaman groaned. "Uh-oh! I've seen what happens when they drink too much whiskey. They barge about, complaining and picking fights."

Sounds just like Titch, I thought. But I didn't say it, even though she was scratching fleas out of her ears and flicking them all over my tail.

Reed staggered through the camp and began hollering at Captain Lewis. Newman shoved Captain Clark so hard he almost fell in the fire.

"Don't let those young pups challenge your authority!" I barked at Lewis. "You're pack leader, by jiminy! Show them who's boss."

Lewis seemed to get the message and ordered the troublemakers out of the camp. But just when the situation seemed to be under control, two of Larocque's men stormed up to their leader, pushing Reed and Newman ahead of them. "Just caught these scoundrels red-handed," one of them shouted. He was waving a bundle of furs and a pouch of coins.

It was clear those troublemakers had been caught stealing.

All of a sudden, Reed lunged forward and punched Captain Lewis. York jumped up and pulled him to the ground. One of Larocque's men took a swipe at Newman. He missed and hit his friend on the nose. Suddenly all the men in both packs were on their feet. Some threw punches. Others threw cups or plates or rocks. The stink of rage swirled in the air with the whiskey fumes. It made my fur prickle. Seaman flew to Lewis's side and growled fiercely at Reed. I ran to join York. I couldn't make sense of this fight, but York was my human now. It was my duty to protect him. I snarled at anyone who came too close.

"Stop!" Maia hissed at Seaman. "You're

making it worse. You should take your own advice, mister. The part about knowing when to hold back." She cuffed my ear with her paw. "You too, Trevor! You can't solve *every* problem by rushing in and biting things."

I heard Titch's voice behind me. "Biting things usually works for me, Princess Fluffybutt. Although, I must admit, biting *humans* never ends well. Believe me, I've been there."

"Maia's right," Newton shouted over the clamor. "We should be using our brains, not our teeth."

I wasn't so sure. Some of the men were reaching for their guns and knives.

How were *brains* going to stop bullets and blades?

15

SHADOWS ON THE WALL

We need to make the humans forget about fighting," said Newton. "We need a *distraction.*"

"My point exactly," said Maia. "One distraction coming right up." She flipped up onto her back legs and began to skip and twirl. The beads and shells and feathers that Sacagawea had braided into her fur jangled and fluttered as she moved. A few of the men stopped to watch. One or two picked up their fiddles and began to play again. But others were still brawling.

"Come on!" Maia called to us. "Join in!"

Titch snorted. "Do I *look* like a dancer?"

Maia did another leaping twirl. "You don't have to dance. Just lie down in a row."

We all did as we were told. Even Baxter, who was quivering like a rattlesnake tail.

Maia jumped over us. Once, twice, then again, backward. "Now, on your backs with your paws in the air," she said. She hopped from one to the next, using us as stepping-stones. When she got to Seaman's big webbed paws, she did a backflip.

The distraction was working. The fiddle players struck up another tune. Most of the men had begun to laugh and clap along. But a few of the younger ones were still brandishing their guns and knives. We needed a showstopper . . .

But what could we do? I stared at Maia, frantically trying to think of something. As she danced and pranced in the firelight, so did her long, flickering shadow on the buffalo-skin wall of the tent behind her. That's what gave me my idea. I whispered the plan to Seaman. He agreed. I quickly dragged a branch from the stack of firewood and dropped it at York's feet. It took a while, but at last he understood. He climbed up on the branch.

Seaman reared up on his back legs beside him.

"Help!" bellowed York. "It's a bear!"

Seaman roared and swiped at him with a massive paw.

On the wall, a shadow-puppet bear attacked a shadow-puppet man in a shadow-puppet tree.

"Help!" cried York once more.

I barked and ran at Seaman, pulling him away by his long, shaggy tail.

"It's Hero to the rescue!" York cried.

All the men cheered as they watched our shadows acting out the grizzly bear attack. Some of them picked up the guns they'd been fighting with and used their shadows to pretend to shoot the bear. Every time they shouted, "Bang!" Seaman pretended to be hit. He staggered about until, at last, he rolled over, playing dead.

The men shouted for more. We must have performed that play a hundred times! But the distraction had finally worked. They'd forgotten all about the fight.

"Good job today, Maia," I said, as we curled up by the embers of the fire. "Your dance routine kept the humans out of trouble."

"How about *your* routine, Captain Hero?" said Titch. "That bear act was a stroke of genius. Totally nuts, but genius all the same!"

"It was fun," said Maia. Then she sighed. "I miss my dance classes with Ayesha . . . Let's go home tomorrow, Trevor."

I glanced at Seaman, who was already snoring. He'd been telling me all day that his back leg was still weak. I had suspected he was faking it a little, because he wanted us to stay longer. After his showstopping performance as the Ferocious Bear, I was now certain; there was nothing wrong with his legs!

First thing next morning, I called the pack together to leave.

Newton, Baxter, and Titch gathered around.

But Maia was nowhere to be seen.

16

VANISHED

We searched every corner of the camp.

Maia wasn't in any of the tents. She wasn't in any of the boats.

She hadn't gone with Sacagawea to collect firewood.

She wasn't under the pine trees, where Larocque and his men had tied up their horses. They had left before first light. All that remained were clumps of soft green horse dung.

We howled Maia's name until the men yelled at us to stop. My heart was turning inside out. Had she been taken by a wolf or a coyote? Had she fallen into the river? Maia wasn't just a member of my pack. She was my oldest friend. I'd known her since we were tiny puppies, long before we started going to Happy Paws Farm and met Baxter and Newton.

And now she had vanished.

Seaman ran out from Captain Lewis's tent. "I know what happened. I just heard the men talking. From what I can make out, Captain Clark has given Maia to Larocque as a gift to make up for all the trouble last night."

"He can't do that!" I gulped. "Maia's not a bunch of flowers! She's not his to give!"

Seaman sighed. "I know. But I guess Clark thought she was a wild dog. Like Fang and her pack. He didn't know you pups belong with the *Fly-Ing-Van* nation."

"Maia? *Wild?*" Titch snorted so hard she almost choked. "Since when do wild dogs wear silly little collars with pink sequins?"

"Maybe Captain Clark didn't notice her collar," Newton pointed out. "It kind of blends in with all those beads and feathers in her fur."

"But why would Larocque *want* Maia anyway?" whimpered Baxter. "I know she's smart, but she hates hunting and she's not much of a tracker . . ."

"Larocque doesn't want her for himself," said Seaman. "He's taking her back to the city. He has a lady friend who trains a troupe of dogs to dance and do tricks. He thinks Maia could be famous . . . the star of the show."

"Being made to prance about onstage like a circus poodle!" I spluttered.

"Ladies and gentlemen, boys and girls! It's Princess Fluffybutt, the Perfect Performing Papillon!" barked Titch in a dramatic voice.

"What's the problem? Maia loves showing off. She'll have a ball."

"All *alone*?" I shouted. "In a city far away? Without her human? Without *us*?" I didn't wait to hear any more. I was already racing back to the pine trees where Larocque's horses had been tied up. I had to find Maia and bring her back.

I was in such a hurry I forgot to give the command for the pack to follow.

Luckily, I didn't need to.

Newton, Baxter, Seaman—and even Titch—were right behind me.

17

BRAINSTORM

Larocque's group had not been gone long. Their scent was fresh and strong: the grass, sweat, and dust of the horses; the gunpowder, whiskey, and smoke of the men; and the half-digested-fish-gut stink of the wild dogs tagging along behind them. Even a human could have followed that trail!

"This way!" I shouted.

We ran and ran; through long, swaying

grass and rustling pine woods and patches where wildfires had burned the land to thick black dust. The sun beat down on our backs. Prickly pear spines stabbed our paws. Mosquitoes buzzed in our ears. Half swimming, half wading, we crossed a stream and came at last to the end of the trail.

At the top of the steep bank were the remains of a campfire. The horses stood nearby, heads down, munching at the grass.

But there was no sign of the men or the dogs.

There was no sign of Maia.

I heard a bark. At least, I thought I did. It was so soft it could have been a mouse squeak. My ears quivered as I strained to hear over the chirping of crickets and warbling of birds. Yes! There it was again.

Faint, feeble, but definitely a bark! My heart leaping, I spun around and homed in on the sound. There, under a cottonwood tree, hidden by the long grass, I found her. A metal chain had been knotted around her collar. The other end was looped over a branch, high up in the tree.

"Maia!" I cried. "Are you hurt?"

"Trevor!" she croaked, struggling to her

paws. "I'm not hurt. But I've been shouting for help so long I almost lost my voice."

The others raced to my side. "Maia! Thank goodness you're safe," gasped Newton. Baxter leaped on her and gave her a big slobbery lick to the ear.

Even Titch looked happy to see Maia. Not for long! "What happened to Fearsome Fang and her gang?" she grumbled. "Why didn't they help you?"

"They disappeared before we crossed the stream," said Maia. "I guess they got bored of following the humans and went off hunting."

Suddenly Newton's ears pricked up. "*Shhh!* What's that?"

Everyone listened. Sounds of human voices and splashing water were drifting on the breeze from somewhere near the stream.

Seaman sniffed the air. "I reckon they've found themselves a hot spring."

We all looked at one another. We knew we had to rescue Maia before the men came back. Then we looked at the metal chain. We also knew it wouldn't be easy.

Maia peered up through the leaves. "If only I could reach that branch, I could unhook the chain."

Newton frowned, head tipped to one side. "We could build a tower for you to climb," he said. "If we stack up some rocks . . ."

I know Newton is the brains of the pack, but it seemed like a crazy idea to me. But Baxter was already tearing around, looking for rocks. He always listens to Newton. If Newton's next brainstorm was to build a tower of flowers to reach the moon, Baxter would run off in search of daisies. Suddenly all my worrying about Maia turned to anger. "How did you let yourself be *given away as a gift*?" I snapped. "What kind of nincompoop does that?"

Maia hung her head. "Captain Clark and Larocque were being so nice about my dancing. I thought they were going to give me a prize or something. Next thing I knew, Larocque had bundled me into a basket and slung me onto the back of his horse. I'm sorry . . ."

I felt bad for being so mean. "No, I'm sorry. It wasn't your fault . . ."

Thud, thud, thud!

Titch had started butting her head against the cottonwood tree.

"What the blazes are you *doing*?" asked Seaman, who was helping Baxter and Newton stack up the rocks.

"Knocking down the tree, of course," Titch said between thuds. "Brainbox Newton is overthinking the problem as usual. That tower plan is way too slow."

Titch was right. The men could return at any moment. The tower of rocks was still nowhere near the branch. But the knock-the-tree-down plan was no better. The trunk was even more solid than Titch's head. I ran in frantic circles, trying to figure it out. *Stay calm*, I told myself. *Assess the situation. There has to be a way!* If Maia was tied with a rope, I could bite through it. But even terrier teeth are no match for a metal chain. And the chain was tied so tightly to Maia's collar. No dog could untie that knot . . .

Maia's collar! That was it.

Suddenly I knew what to do.

18

TEAMWORK

I couldn't bite through the metal chain, but I *could* bite through a little pink collar.

I grabbed it in my teeth and tried to rip it apart. But sequins are surprisingly tough.

"I'll help!" cried Baxter. "I can chew through anything."

Together we gnawed at the collar like starving coyotes. Suddenly it gave way. We fell back, knocking over the tower of rocks.

Maia sprang free, shaking the torn collar from her neck.

I spat out a sequin.

Seaman and Titch cheered.

Newton looked at the half-made tower and smiled. "Just this once, I reckon that's a win for teeth over brains."

Maia laughed and nudged my nose with hers. "Thank you . . ."

Suddenly she fell silent. We all heard it at the same time. *Voices, footsteps . . .* "Doggone it!" muttered Seaman. We'd been working so hard to free Maia that we hadn't heard the humans until they were almost upon us.

"Retreat!" I yelled.

Larocque and his men chased after us. Newton and Baxter were fast enough to get away. Seaman and Maia and I could probably have made it, too. But Titch was slower. She has a leg missing, after all, and she was still dizzy from head-butting the tree. I glanced back over my shoulder. The men were throwing stones. One hit Titch's tail. Another missed her head by a whisker. *Never Leave a Dog Behind.* I had to go back for her.

But as I turned, Titch stopped running. She swung around, lowered her head, and charged at the humans.

"Titch!" yelled Seaman. "Come back! You'll get yourself killed."

I could hardly bear to watch. But at the last moment, Titch swerved.

It wasn't the men she was charging at.

It was the horses!

The terrified animals reared up, squealing and pawing at the sky, and pulling the bush they were tied to straight out of the ground. Then they bolted, mud flying from their hooves. The men raced after them. All but one. He turned back, raising his gun.

"Look out, Titch!" I cried. But she was whooping in victory so loud she didn't hear me.

I closed my eyes, braced for the crack of the gun. But when the noise came, it wasn't a gunshot. It was an explosion of yipping and snarling. The wild dogs flew out from the bushes and knocked the man off his feet. The gun fell from his hands into the long grass. "Run for it!" howled Fang. "I told you humans were trouble!"

I took a last look back. The man was sitting up, trying to figure out what just hit him. The wild dogs had already slipped away into the undergrowth. "Thank you!" I shouted. And then, "Hurry up, Titch!"

We didn't stop running until we were on the bank of the Missouri. We waded into the water to drink and cool down. Titch nudged my side. "So, Captain Hero. How was *that* for a distraction? Horses love a drama. You can always rely on them to overreact."

"You were awesome," said Baxter.

"And so was Fang," said Maia, her voice still croaky.

Titch shrugged. "I guess she helped a little. But I had it covered."

"Of course you did!" said Newton, laughing.

I nudged Titch back. "Good job, Titch. Great teamwork."

I laughed, too. I never thought I would say the words *Titch* and *teamwork* in the same breath.

19

THE PARTING OF WAYS

It was time to say goodbye. Seaman was heading back upriver to the Lewis and Clark camp. We were continuing down-river to the van—and home.

I was sad to leave. York was a good man. Hunting with him had been fun. But I was happy, too. I belong with Old Jim. I knew that Newton and Maia and Baxter felt the same way. They longed to be home, but they would miss Sacagawea and the baby and Captains Lewis and Clark.

I thought Titch might decide to stick around with Seaman. She had no human family to miss. "Fearsome Fang was right about one thing," she said. "Humans are trouble." But Titch *was* missing tacos and hot sauce and tuna cat food. "Even buffalo meat gets boring after a while," she said. "So long, Duckzilla," she called after Seaman. "It's been a blast."

"Goodbye, Titch. I hope we meet again soon to swap more stories." Seaman smiled

and shook his head. "Although I can't figure out how you've had so many doggone adventures when you're still just a pup."

Titch grinned. "That, my woolly friend, really *is* magic!"

Two days' walk brought us back to the van. It still looked like a willow tree. A pair of crows were bickering in its branches. But there was no mistaking that scent. *Metal. Rubber. Gasoline. Roads.*

Baxter spotted his tennis ball floating among the reeds and jumped in to fetch it.

I pressed my nose against the tree. *Pop!* It turned into the van again.

I took a last look across the Missouri River. The sun was setting behind the mountains. The plains glowed in the fiery

light. A flock of geese flew low over the water. I was going to miss this place.

Inside the van, Newton hopped up into the driver's seat and stared down at the control panel. The lights still made the pattern:

1 8 0 5

Maia closed the back doors and settled down on the bed to nibble the beads and shells out of her fur.

I gave the command. "Take us home, Newton!"

Newton poked at the control panel. Nothing happened.

Baxter peered over Newton's shoulder, dripping muddy water from the tennis ball.

The lights flashed.

The van rumbled and shook and rose into the air.

20

ALL CLEAR

Clatter, thud, scrape. It was another bumpy landing.

We jumped out of the van. We were back in the barn at Happy Paws Farm. It was just as we left it. Inventions hanging on the racks. Pigeons roosting on the rafters.

I peeped out the barn door. The yard was empty. Rain splashed into puddles. I gave the all-clear signal and we ran to the house. Rather slowly. We were old again, and the spring had gone out of our legs.

Titch shambled off down the road in search of garbage cans and bowls of cat food. "So long, old-timers," she called. "Until the next road trip!"

"What's that she said?" Newton rubbed his ear with his paw. "Doggone hearing's gone again," he grumbled. He sounded just like Seaman!

We followed Baxter through the dog flap and curled up by the fire.

I woke to a familiar smell. *Newspapers. Hard candies. Soap.*

There was a familiar sound, too; the *tap, tap, tap* of a walking stick. My ears pricked up. A man's voice was calling, "Trevor!" At first, I didn't answer. I'd gotten so used to being Hero, I almost forgot that meant me!

Old Jim! I ran to meet him. I leaped at his legs, wagging my tail like crazy. "Don't worry, Jim!" I barked. "I'm back on duty now. Anything to report while I was away?"

Old Jim laughed and rubbed my ears, just the way he always does. He said something to Baxter's human, Lucy, who was with him. "I've only been gone a couple of hours! You'd think Trevor hadn't seen me for days!" He picked a prickly pear spine out of my fur and gave me a puzzled look.

Lucy looked up from hugging Baxter. Her hands were streaked with mud from his fur. Then she petted Maia and frowned. She'd clearly noticed that the pink sequined collar was missing. She picked a stray bead from Maia's fur. "I don't understand. They've just been snoozing by the fire all afternoon."

Old Jim nodded slowly. He bent down and patted Newton. Grass seeds scattered from his fur. Old Jim looked back at me and then at Lucy. "Do you ever wonder what these old dogs get up to when we're not looking?"

The only one of their words I understood was *dogs*.

But I could tell Old Jim was happy, so I jumped up and licked his nose to tell him I was happy, too.

AUTHOR'S NOTE

Trevor, Baxter, Maia, Newton, and Titch are fictional characters. But the dogs they meet on their travels through time really existed. Their adventures together are inspired by actual events; events in which the real dogs played a crucial part.

Seaman, a large Newfoundland, accompanied Meriwether Lewis and William Clark and the Corps of Discovery on their expedition along the Missouri River and across the Rocky Mountains to the Pacific Ocean. This would be an important trading route for President Jefferson and the United States. They set out in May 1804 and reached the coast in November 1805.

We know a lot about this epic journey because Lewis, Clark, and several other members of the expedition kept detailed journals—journals that we can still read today. The other human characters in this story were real people, too. York was a slave who belonged to Captain Clark's family. Sacagawea was a young Shoshone woman who joined the expedition as their interpreter (and she did have a baby!). The "troublemakers" Moses Reed and John Newman were both members of the expedition who really were punished for bad behavior, including desertion and mutiny. François-Antoine Larocque was a trader for the North West Company (a Canadian fur-trading business)—and an explorer in his own right—who met Lewis and Clark on their journey.

The dangers that Seaman and the time dogs face in my story are based on real events. Lewis and Clark's men had several encounters with grizzly bears. Antelope swam across the river to escape from wolves, and Seaman really was bitten very badly on the leg by a beaver. A rogue buffalo charged through the camp in the middle of the night. One of the boats was caught up in a gust of wind and almost sank. Lewis describes how Sacagawea saved supplies from being washed away. An important compass was lost (and found again!)—although in real life, this did not happen in the boat accident. It happened when several of the group were on foot and they were caught in a rainstorm on the river. They had a narrow escape and some of their possessions were damaged or washed away (including the baby's carrier). Coyotes, wildcats, rattlesnakes, hailstones, grass fires, and mudslides were all real hazards. The journals often mention the irritations of mosquitoes and prickly pear spines. Similarly, there are several reports of the men having rather too much whiskey and getting into fights.

The real events that inspired this book happened over many months. For the purposes of the story, I have squashed the time dogs' adventures into a few days in the summer of 1805. At this time, the expedition was traveling along the Missouri River in what is now Montana. However, the locations in the book do not correspond to specific places, and I have imported some events that happened earlier in the journey. Reed and Newman had both been dismissed and sent back to St. Louis by the spring of 1805. The meeting with Larocque and his party took place earlier in the expedition, at Fort Mandan, where the men spent the winter of 1804–05. Although the two groups spent some time together, and there were some misunderstandings, I invented the incident in which the fight broke out between them. Similarly, as far as I know, Larocque didn't have a lady friend who trained dogs for the stage!